O ne hundred percent certifiably, undeniably, royal pup seeks an equally majestic owner with an imperial dwelling and a true heart. Qualified applicants of proper pedigree only

PLEASE!

-Mr. Allbite Snifferson Tall, proprietor

Henley

By Julie Muszynski

Glitterati

INCORPORATED

New York, New York

For my Henley

First published in the United States of America in 2005 by Glitterati Incorporated 225 Central Park West New York, New York 10024

First edition, 2005
Hardcover ISBN 1-57687-253-x

Printed and bound in China by Hong Kong Graphics & Printing Ltd.

10 9 8 7 6 5 4 3 2 1

Distributed in North America by powerHouse Books, a division of powerHouse Cultural Entertainment, Inc. 68 Charlton Street, New York, New York 10014 telephone 212 604 9074, fax 212 366 5247 email: Henley@powerHouseBooks.com web site: www.powerHouseBooks.com

Design by Julie Muszynski & Belinda Hellinger
Production Photographer Tim Thayer

Hand Calligraphy by Sheryl D. Nelson

I would
like to
thank
and give
credit to
Marta,
Minju,
and
Belinda.
I would
also like
to give a
special
thank you
to
Elizabeth
Sullivan.

Also...

Mom
Dad
Daphne
Lila
Frank
Becky

and...

Ophelia

Please
remember
that, no
matter
what,
whether
adopting
an adorable
mutt or
pedigree
pup, all
dogs deserve
boundless
love and
attention,
for what they
give back is
more than
one can
mention.

This is the story of Henley, the most extraordinary pup ever to have lived at the Sweetie Pie Pet Shop in New York City. The shop's proprietor, the most debonair, Mr. Allbite Snifferson Tall, took good care of him and everyone who stopped by admired him.

"Henley, you are going to be a star! Destined for greatness, that I'm sure! Once we find you the perfect home, there is one thing for certain every good dog must know. It's not about your pedigree or that you come from royalty, the most important thing, you see, is to always remember your LOYALTY!" said Mr. Allbite Snifferson Tall.

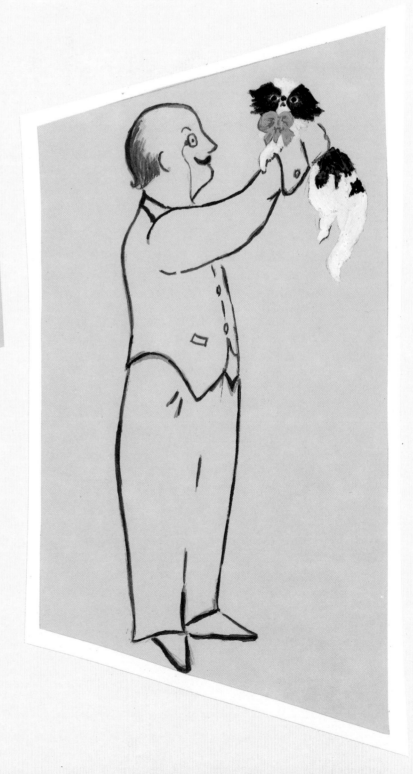

One morning, the elegant and very accessorized Ms. Lulu Ziminski, fashion maven extraordinaire who was world-famous for her flair, entered the Sweetie Pie Pet Shop.

And before Mr. Allbite Snifferson Tall could say a word, she threw her arms up into the air and quickly announced, "I'd like to inquire about this so called royal pup that you have advertised in the window of your shop. That flirtatious fellow caught my eye just as I was passing by."

Mr. Allbite Snifferson Tall took one look at her and immediately replied," Why, of course, Madame." He walked over to his precious pet and proudly exclaimed, "Please allow me to introduce you to the finest canine you may ever meet. Ms. Lulu Ziminski, this is HENLEY!"

When Ms. Lulu Ziminski saw Henley, she gasped with delight and crossed her bejeweled hands over her heart. "My! What a madly, marvelous, and magnificent creature! And so unique! What on earth is he?"

"This teeny, tiny pup is extremely rare," said Mr. Allbite Snifferson Tall." Henley is a Japanese Chin. A gem in the rough of pups, my dear!"

Mr. Allbite Snifferson Tall straightened his red silk bowtie and continued, "Why, this is no ordinary dog, I assure you! His breed is chic! Privileged! Divine! It's unlikely you will ever find a specimen this fine."

Mr. Allbite Snifferson Tall walked to his soaring bookcase and pulled down an enormous, old, leather-bound book with gold edges. Pointing to a very complicated chart, he said to Lulu, "You see? Look here,"

Henley is a descendent of le chien lion!

The lion dog!

The King of dogs!

Bred exclusively for nobility, his lineage is filled with royalty!"

Ms. Lulu was certainly impressed, for she, too, had a royal past; her great great uncle was said to be the esteemed Prince Ziminik Ziminski.

160° 180° 160° 140° 120° 100° 80° 60° 40° 20° 0°

80°

ARCTIC OCEAN

GREENLAND
(Den.)

RUSSIA

U.S

ALASKA

NORTH

CANADA

AMERICA

Arctic Circle

ICELAND

60°

UNITED
KINGDOM

IRELAND

NORTH

UNITED

STATES

40°

NORTH

ATLANTIC

FRANC

SPAIN

PACIFIC

PORT

MOROCCO

ALGE

OC

Tropic Line

BAHAMAS

MEXICO

CUBA

BELIZE

HAITI DOM. REP.

PUERTO RICO

W. SAHARA

U.S.

(cer)

OCEAN

20°

JAM.

HON.

1

MAUR.

SENEGAL

13

MALI

GUAT.

EL SAL.

DOMINICA

BARBADOS

GAMB

14

17 F

NIC.

2

GUINEA

15 16

CENTRAL

C.R.

VEN.

GUY

LIBERIA

PAN.

3

SUR.

GHANA

AMERICA

COLOMBIA

FR.G.

Equator

TOGO

ECU.

2C

0°

KIRIBA

SOUTH

PERU

BRAZIL

SAMOA

AMERICA

BOL

20°

TONGA

South Tropic Line
(Tropic of Capricorn)

PAR

S O U T H

SOUTH

UR

T I

40°

CHILE

ARGENTINA

PACIFIC

N

OCEAN

60°

Antarctic Circle

ANTARCT

OCEAN

80°

U.S

60°

RUSSIA

EUROPE

SWEDEN

FINLAND

EST. LAT.
LITH. POL. BEL.
GER.
UKR.
ROM.
BULG.
TURKEY
GR.
SYR.
TUN.
IRAQ IRAN
ITALY
JOR.
IBR.
LIBYA
EGYPT
SAUDI ARABIA
OMAN
YEMEN

KAZAKH.

ASIA

MONGOLIA

CHINA

AFGH.

PAK.

NEPAL

INDIA

MYANMAR
THAI.
CAMB. VIET.

N. KOR.
S. KOR.

JAPAN

NORTH

PACIFIC

OCEAN

40°

20°

TAIWAN

PHILIPPINES

BRUNEI
MALAYSIA

NIGER CHAD SUDAN
G. CAM.
GABON
NGO DEM. REP. OF THE CONGO
NGOLA
ZAMBIA
MBIA
BOTS
SOUTH AFRICA

ETH.
SOMALIA
KENYA
TANZANIA
MAL.
MOZAM.
ZIM
SWAZILAND
LESOTHO

SEYCHELLES
COMOROS
MADAGASCAR
MAURITIUS

SRI LANKA
MALDIVES

INDIAN

OCEAN

INDONESIA

E. TIMOR

AUSTRALIA

KIR.

0°

FIJI

NEW ZEALAND

20°

40°

"Did you know," Mr. Allbite Snifferson Tall said, as he pulled out his customized Dog World Map, a gift from his dear friend Baron Bouviers des Flandres, director of the So Frou Frou Gallery of Art. "Henley's great ancestors came from Japan. In fact, many of his royal cousins came from England."

60°

C A

Japan,
the home of glorious

tea gardens and ⭐ Tokyo

GIANT goldfish!

JAPAN

JAPAN—a name signifying the Land of the Rising Sun—bears a rising sun on its flag. Its exact origin is lost in antiquity, but some historians say it was used as early as 702 A.D. Because Japan lies in the Far East and is the first to greet the morning sun, the flag is a beautiful and fitting emblem of the Japanese Empire.

The flag is the pride of every land

No. 23

Turning back to his book, Mr. Allbite Snifferson Tall said, "Ah, yes, let's see, Japan...

"The ancient relatives of this petite little prince were, by far, the favorite royal companions and friends to many of the emperors of Japan. These precocious pets were never ever meant to be in the dreadfully dull possession of a commoner.

JAPAN

Princess Cherry Blossom

Little Ming & Sing Sing

"Why, they often warmed the laps of the ladies in the Imperial Palace!"

England!

GREAT BRITAIN

THE first English flag was the red cross of St. George. When Scotland and England were united the flag of St. Andrew of Scotland—a white diagonal cross on a blue ground—was combined with that of England. With the addition of Ireland to the British Empire, the flag of St. Patrick—a red diagonal cross on a white ground—was joined with the other two to form the present British flag.

The flag is the pride of every land

No. 5

LONDON 1959

The land of Kings and Queens London and scones and tea!

ROYAL MAIL

1

POSTAGE PAID

GREAT BRITAIN

W7047

CENTRAL
LONDON

...esty, Queen Victoria, was wildly
...her devilish little Chins, but it was
...onally fashionable daughter-in-law,
...incess Alexandra who became so
...She acquired twenty-six!"

Punch	Lord Winslow
Facey	Patience
ttle Marvel	LadyHazel
Birdie	Pirouette
Cissie	Little Odelette
Bliss	Lady Agatha
Barclay	Tiggy
rd Sheffield	Marlowe
Hastings	Teddy
Piper	Sir Valentine
Darling	Dainty
Tuesday	Little Landseer
H.R.H. Queenie	Prince

Japanese Spaniel.

ALEXANDRA

Lord Sheffield
Hastings
Piper
Darling
Tuesday
HRH Queenie

Marlowe
Teddy
Sir Valentine
Dainty
Little Landseer
Prince

Facey

Birdie

Barclay & Bliss

Dainty & Patience

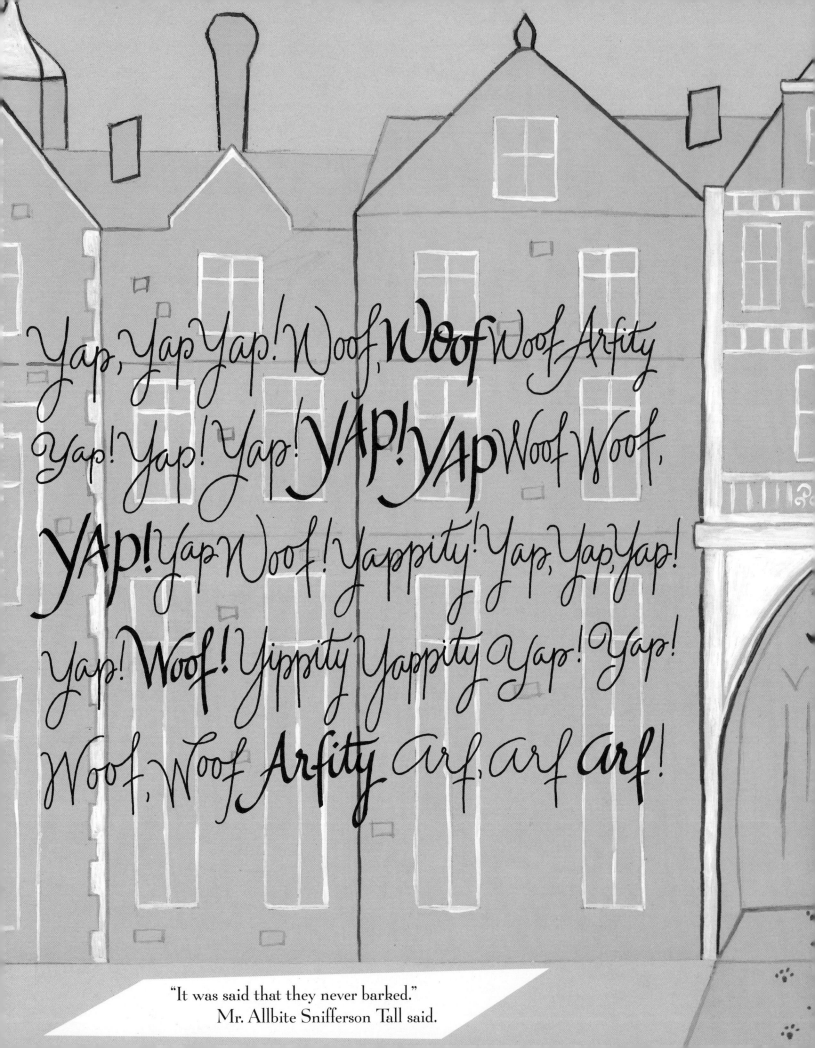

"It was said that they never barked."
Mr. Allbite Snifferson Tall said.

Yap Yap YAP YAP Yap WOOf Yappity

Arf, Arf, Arf! Yap! Woof! Yappity! Yap, Yap

Woof Arfity Arf Arf Arf! Yap! Yap! YAP

Woof, Woof, WOOF Arfity, Arf Arf Arf!

Yap! Yap! Yap Yap! YAP! YAP! Woof

"Well, most of the time...."

Little Marvel

The Royal Children

"Oooooooh! He's absolutely adorable and so royal! The cutest thing I've ever seen! Would you mind terribly if I held him please?" she said to Mr. Allbite Snifferson Tall.

With that Mr. Allbite Snifferson Tall carefully picked Henley up and gently placed him into Ms. Lulu Ziminski's glittering hands.

As she held him, Henley batted his huge brown eyes, wagged his little white tail, tapped her lightly with his dainty paw, and then delicately licked her on the cheek.

In that moment, they fell in love.

PET PAPERS

An Immunization Record and Valuable Documents Folder Pertaining To

Name	Henley	Date of Birth	3/30
			(Month-Yr.)

Breed *Japanese Chin* Sex *Male*

Owner *Ms. Lulu Ziminski*

Address *One Pedigree Place*

City *New York*

Certificate of Birth

SWEETIE PIE PET SHOP
1 in 1,000,000 FIFTH AVENUE
NEW YORK, NEW YORK 10021

NAME: HENLEY
GLORIOUS DATE OF ADOPTION: May 23
LUCKY ADOPTEE: Ms. Lulu Ziminski
HANDSOME SALESMAN: Mr. Allbite Snifferson Tall
REGAL BREED: Japanese Chin
GENDER: Male
BLESSED DATE OF BIRTH: March 30
SIRE: Take a Chance on Me
DAM: Tuttie Fruitie

I HEREBY AGREE TO LOVE, ADORE, SPOIL, AND
TAKE CARE OF THIS PUPPY FOREVER.

SIGNATURE: *Lulu Ziminski* DATE: 5.23

How to care for your dog

"NO MOTHER TO GUIDE THEM"

Sergeant's DOG BOOK

by

D. E. BUCKINGHAM. V. M. D.

Gracious gift from Mr. Allbite Snifferson Tall

In the morning, weather permitting, of course, Ms. Lulu and Henley enjoyed their breakfast on the terrace facing east.

And so on that most glorious day, in the most fabulous city in the world,

Please do

Henley went to live with Ms. Lulu Ziminski at the extremely posh and very exclusive One Pedigree Place.

In the evening, beneath the midnight blue sky, Ms. Lulu and Henley had the most extravagant cocktail parties on the terrace facing west.

The glittering and glamorous New York penthouse
apartment of Ms. Lulu Ziminski, descendant of Prince
Ziminik Ziminski, and her adoring pet, Henley, a
royal Japanese Chin.

Saturdays, Lulu and Henley got up early and zipped over to the Farmers Market in Union Square Park.

After all, it is the most delicious place to be!

T ogether the two had
so much fun!...

Riding up Bark Avenue.

Pampering at the Elizabeth Arfden Salon.

Yapping on the telephone, well, most of the time.

Reading the Sunday New Yorkie *Times*.

Rose gardening on the terrace with
trowels from Jackson & Barkins.

Traveling abroad in style on Pet Blue.

Evening strolls in the latest Poochi Couture.

Ommmmmmmmm at Doga.

Dining on the finest filet mignon at the Fur Seasons.

Bathing in the paw-footed tub.

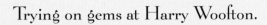

Trying on gems at Harry Woofton.

But, most importantly, besides
anything else, they loved each other.

One spring afternoon, Lulu and Henley stopped into Bergdorf Goodman for a few lovely baubles and such and, of course, more of that fabulous purple gift ribbon that Henley loves to play with so much.

When they entered the store they were suddenly surprised, something incredible was happening inside.

...ng and flashing, terrifically
...d up in beautiful clothes,
...v around, zipping up zippers
...the middle of it all was
...do d'Eduardo, whose face

...s she blew him a big kiss.

...ably replied.

...are a

...lous!"
...ey, whose tail

...ulu's Ziminski's
...sed his head
...nced onto

..." shouted the
...ner.

...dearing stare...

...gal composure!

...wsitively brilliant

a star!"

Bright lights and cameras were popp
tall girls were roaming about all dresse
people everywhere were rushing mad
and tying up bows, and smack dab in
Lulu's good friend Eduardo d'Eduar
was bright red!

"D A R L I N G!" Lulu exclaimed

"D A R L I N G!" Eduardo fashion

"I am simply frantic! Flabbergasted!
Flummoxed! These frivolous frocks
frightening flop!

"Why, D A R L I N G, you're fabu
Eduardo exclaimed pointing to Hen
started to wag.

With that, Henley leapt out of Ms. L
sparkling hands, rai
proudly and pra
the set.

"That face.
photograp

"That en

That re

You're pa
Henley!

It's a wrap...

HENLEY, You are going to be

And, sure enough, the photographer was right. Virtually it happened overnight. The catalogue was such an immediate and tremendous success that Henley had instantly become FAMOUS!...

He was the first dog ever to judge the Westminster Dog Show.

Everyone on Seventh Avenue wanted to dress him.

He was invited to play catch with the Yankees.

He had a permanent box seat at every performance of "Cats" on Broadway.

The *pupperazzi* followed his every move.

And he rang the bell at the New York Stock Exchange.

NYSE

October 12

Henley was invited to all the movie premieres at the Ziegfeld Theater...

He was the only dog allowed at the Metropolitan Museum of Art.

The mayor gave him the key to the city.

Everyone wanted his pawtograph.

He lit the Christmas tree at Rockefeller Center...

and dropped the New Year's Eve Ball in Times Square.

It was said that Eloise's mother was so intrigued when she came across Henley in her Bergdorf Goodman catalogue, she immediately rang up the store and tried to buy him for her daughter. BUT when she was told he just wasn't for sale, she quickly sent out a personal invitation for Henley to join Eloise and her dog, Weenie, for an afternoon of fun at the landmark Plaza Hotel.

"HENLEY seen..."

Page 6

Meow Mix

December 2, 2004

Tails were wagging last night when Henley the "Hotdog" of the moment was spotted attending The Bow Wow Wow Ball, the biggest canine charity event in the entire world! Our feline spy reports that Henley proudly spent his entire 50-bone paycheck on the magnificent portrait, Glover, taken by the legendary canine photographer, William Wegman. Rumor has it Mr. Wegman was so impressed… He gave Henley his autograph!

The Plug

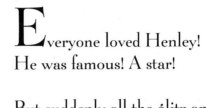

Everyone loved Henley!
He was famous! A star!

But suddenly all the glitz and
glamour galore lost its allure.

Something was missing, something very dear to his heart.
But just what was it that Henley
had simply forgot? He'd go to
Central Park.

Balto will know the answer.

Heading home, Henley realized
that what Balto said was true.
Henley now knew what to do.

No matter what came his way...

Ms. Lulu would always

ABSOLUTELY,

PAWSITIVELY,

INDISPUTABLY,

IRRUFFUTABLY,

AND

TRULY

BE...

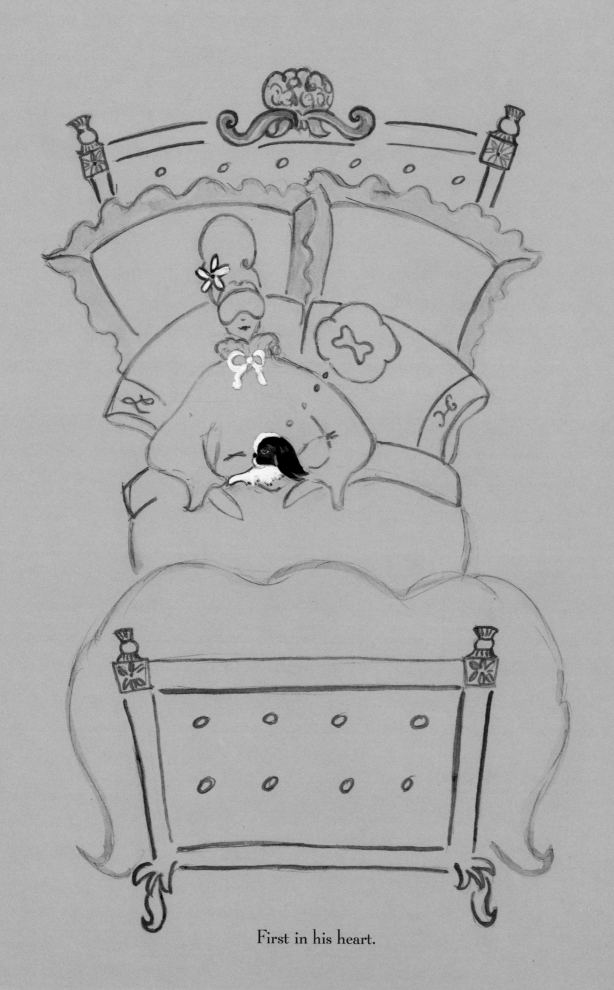

First in his heart.